IGLOOK'S SEAL

Written and illustrated by

BERNARD WISEMAN

Weekly Reader Children's Book Club presents

DODD, MEAD & COMPANY

NEW YORK

Graphics Assistant: Susan N. Wiseman

Weekly Reader Children's Book Club Edition

Library of Congress Cataloging in Publication Data

Wiseman, Bernard.
    Iglook's seal.

SUMMARY: A little Eskimo boy takes a baby seal
home to be his pet rather than kill it.
    [1. Seals (Animals)—Fiction. 2. Eskimos—Fic-
tion] I. Title.
PZ7.W7802Ig   [E]   76-23410
ISBN 0-396-07396-4

Iglook was asleep.
His father shook him.
"Wake up, my son," he said.
"Today you hunt with me."

Iglook's mother said,
"He is only six years old."

His father laughed.
"I was younger on my first hunt."

Iglook's mother sliced some blubber.
She said, "Here is food."

They all ate the whale fat.
Then it was time to hunt.

Iglook and his father put on sealskin
boots, fur parkas, and fur mittens.

Iglook's father smiled.
"I made something," he said.
He gave Iglook a small harpoon.

"Now let us go," his father said.
And they crawled
out of their snow house.

They hitched the dogs to the sled.
Iglook's father yelled, "MUSH!"
The dogs pulled the sled fast.

Soon they came to the ice.

They left the sled.
Iglook's father said,
"We will not walk on the ice.
We will crawl.
Seals will think we are just seals.
They will not be afraid of us."

They crawled across the ice.
Iglook's father pointed.
"There," he whispered,
"I think I see a seal."

Iglook stood up
to get a better look.

The seal saw Iglook.
It saw he was not a seal.
It dived into a hole in the ice.

"I am sorry," Iglook said.
His father said,
"We will find another seal."

They did not find one seal.
They found two seals—
a big one and a little one.
Iglook's father whispered,
"You cannot throw your harpoon
from here. We must crawl closer."

They crawled too close.
The big seal saw they were not seals.
It barked at the little seal.
Both seals began to hop
to a hole in the ice.

"Quick!" Iglook's father cried.
"Throw your harpoon! At the BIG one!"
Iglook jumped up and threw his harpoon.

The big seal dived into the hole.
The harpoon hit the ice.

The little seal was still hopping
to the hole. Iglook's father
ran fast and got there first.

"Pick up your harpoon," he told Iglook.
"Aim well. This seal cannot get away."

Iglook lifted his harpoon.
But, he did not throw it.

"Well?" his father cried.
"What are you waiting for?"
Iglook said, "This seal is
too small. It is just a baby."

"We must eat," his father said.
And he lifted his harpoon.

Iglook jumped between his
father and the baby seal.
"No, father, NO," he cried.
"Let us eat only BIG ones."

"Listen to me," said his father.
"The mother seal has gone away.
This baby seal cannot drink her milk.
And it is too young to eat fish.
It will starve.
Or a polar bear will eat it."

"It will not!" Iglook cried.
He picked up the baby seal
and carried it to the sled.

Iglook carried the baby seal
into his house. His mother said,
"Ah! You bring something!
You have hunted well."

Iglook put the seal on the snow floor.
His mother cried, "But it still moves!"

His father said,
"It is no wonder it moves.
Our son did not throw his harpoon."

Iglook's mother laughed.
"See how it sniffs and looks about.
It is like a little dog."

"It is not a little dog,"
said Iglook's father.
"It is a baby seal.
It is too young to eat fish.
We have no milk for it.
It will starve."

Iglook asked, "Cannot a
mother dog give it milk?"

"A dog would eat the seal,"
said his father.

Iglook's mother put fish
and snow in a pot.
She cooked some fish soup.
The baby seal smelled it.
Then it licked up all the soup.

"Well," Iglook's father said,
"so it will not starve.
But you, my son, must catch its food.
I must hunt to feed us."

Iglook patted the seal's head.
"I will try to catch what he needs.
Now he needs a name.
I will call him Sulak."

The next morning Iglook
went with his father again.
His father said,
"I must go and hunt.
You go find a hole in the ice.
Use this fish hook and line.
Catch fish for your seal."

Iglook stuck a piece of blubber
on the fish hook. He lowered it
into a hole in the ice.

He felt a little tug on
the line. He pulled the line up.
There was no fish on the hook.

Iglook lowered his fish hook
into the hole again. This time
he waited for a strong pull.

Then he pulled the line up.
At the end of it was a big fish!
Iglook had caught food for his seal.

That night Sulak ate
another pot of fish soup.
Iglook said, "You see, father?
I can catch what he needs."
Iglook's father laughed.
"He will soon eat more."

And Sulak did.
Each night he ate more soup.
Soon Sulak began to eat fish.
And each night he ate
more fish than the night before.

Iglook had to catch many fish.
He had to catch fish all day long.

People laughed at Iglook.
One old man said, "Catch a WHALE!
Then your seal will not be hungry."

Children teased Iglook. One boy said,
"Iglook catches fish all day. Soon he
will have to catch fish all night, too."

Iglook's mother said,
"My son, people laugh at you.
Children tease you.
And you have no time to play."

Iglook's father said,
"You have no time to learn to hunt.
All you do is catch fish
for your seal."

One day when Iglook was
catching fish his mother said,
"My son should have time to play.
He should have time to learn to hunt.
I will get rid of this seal."

And she chased Sulak
out of the snow house.

She heard barking and growling.
"Oh!" she cried.
"Dogs are trying to eat Sulak!
I do not want that to happen."
She ran outside
and chased the dogs away.

When Iglook got home he saw
that Sulak had been fighting.

"What happened?" Iglook asked.
His mother told him.
Iglook said, "I will take Sulak
with me when I go fishing."

"You cannot," his father said.
"He is too big now.
He would fill the sled.
There would be no room
for what I catch."

Iglook said, "Please make me a sled."
His father got pieces of wood.
With the pieces of wood and
strips of leather he made a sled.
He gave Iglook four dogs to pull it.

The next morning Iglook
took Sulak to the ice.
Iglook said, "I do not
want you to go away."
He tied a rope around Sulak's neck.

Iglook caught a fish.
Sulak began to bark
and pull at the rope.
He wanted to jump
into the hole in the ice.

Iglook said, "You want to go away.
You want to be with other seals.
I want you to be happy.
I must let you go."

Iglook took the rope off Sulak's neck.
Sulak dived into the hole in the ice.

Iglook started to walk to the sled.
He heard a seal barking.

Iglook looked back. He saw Sulak.
He saw a big fish flopping on the ice.

Iglook ran to Sulak
and hugged him.

"Oh!" Iglook cried.
"You did not want to go away.
You just wanted to catch fish.
You are a seal.
Seals love to catch fish!"

Sulak barked and dived
back into the hole.
He caught fish after fish.

Sulak ate many of the fish,
but not all of them.
He caught too many to eat.
When it was time to go,
there was a big pile
of fish on the ice.

Iglook put the pile of fish
on his sled.
There was no room for Sulak.
Sulak had to sit
on top of the fish.

When people saw all the fish
they were surprised.
"Iglook," an old man said,
"you are a great fisherman!"

"I did not catch the fish,"
Iglook said.
"Sulak, my seal, caught them."
Then Iglook gave fish to everyone.

The next morning there were
still fish left to eat.
Iglook's father did not
have to go hunting.
And Iglook did not
have to go fishing.
He went outside to play.
But, there were no children
to play with.
There was no one outside.

"Father," Iglook cried,
"where is everyone?"

Iglook's father laughed.
"They have gone to the ice.
They have gone to find baby seals.
They all want a seal like yours!"